Note to parents, carers and teachers

Read it yourself is a series of modern stories, favourite characters and traditional tales written in a simple way for children who are learning to read. The books can be read independently or as part of a guided reading session.

Each book is carefully structured to include many high-frequency words vital for first reading. The sentences on each page are supported closely by pictures to help with understanding, and to offer lively details to talk about.

The books are graded into four levels that progressively introduce wider vocabulary and longer stories as a reader's ability and confidence grows.

Ideas for use

- Ask how your child would like to approach reading at this stage. Would he prefer to hear you read the story first, or would he like to read the story to you and see how he gets on?

- Help him to sound out any words he does not know.

- Developing readers can be concentrating so hard on the words that they sometimes don't fully grasp the meaning of what they're reading. Answering the puzzle questions at the end of the book will help with understanding.

For more information and advice on Read it yourself and book banding, visit **www.ladybird.com/readityourself**

Book Band 8

Level 3 is ideal for children who are developing reading confidence and stamina, and who are eager to read longer stories with a wider vocabulary.

Special features:

Wider vocabulary, reinforced through repetition

Detailed pictures for added interest and discussion

Once there was a father who lived with his three sons. When the father died he left each son a gift.

6

7

Longer sentences

Simple story structure

He left his mill to the first son, his donkey to the next son, and his cat to the youngest son.

8

9

Educational Consultant: Geraldine Taylor
Book Banding Consultant: Kate Ruttle

LADYBIRD BOOKS

UK | USA | Canada | Ireland | Australia
India | New Zealand | South Africa

Ladybird Books is part of the Penguin Random House group of companies
whose addresses can be found at global.penguinrandomhouse.com.

ladybird.com

Penguin
Random House
UK

First published 2015
001

Copyright © Ladybird Books Ltd, 2015

Ladybird, Read it yourself and the Ladybird logo are registered or
unregistered trademarks owned by Ladybird Books Ltd

The moral right of the illustrator has been asserted

Printed in China

A CIP catalogue record for this book is available from the British Library

ISBN: 978–0–723–28077–4

Puss in Boots

Illustrated by Laura Barella

Once there was a father who lived with his three sons. When the father died he left each son a gift.

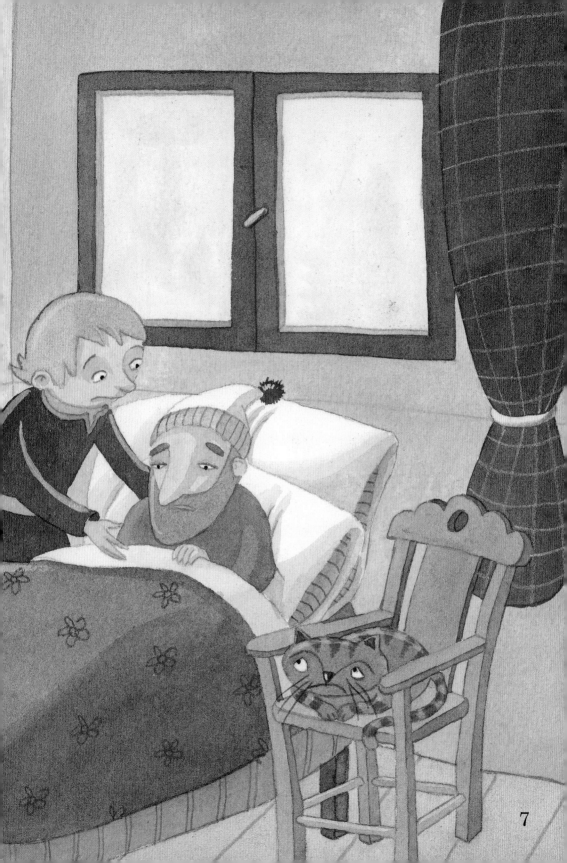

He left his mill to the first son, his donkey to the next son, and his cat to the youngest son.

The youngest son said, "Puss, my brothers can earn money with their gifts. How can we earn some money?"

Puss said, "Master, get me some boots and a bag."

So the boy gave Puss some boots and a bag. First, Puss put on the boots. Then he went out and caught a rabbit in his bag.

Puss took the rabbit to the king.

"Here is a gift from my master," said Puss.

"Thank you Puss, and who is your master?" said the king.

"The Marquis of Carrabas," said Puss.

Soon after, Puss went out with the bag again. This time he caught two partridges. Puss took the partridges to the king.

"Here is a gift of two partridges from my master, the Marquis of Carrabas," said Puss.

"Thank you, Puss in Boots," said the king. "I love to eat partridges."

Soon after, Puss and his master were by a river. Puss saw the king's carriage coming along the road. The king and the princess were in the carriage.

"Master," said Puss, "take off your clothes and jump into the river."

Then Puss ran to the carriage.

"Help me!" said Puss. "My master is in the river, and his clothes have been taken."

23

"We must help the Marquis of Carrabas," said the king. So the king's men helped the boy out of the river.

Then the king said, "We must take you home." And he put the boy into his carriage.

Puss ran along the road. He saw some men working.

"The king is coming," he said. "Say that the Marquis of Carrabas is your master."

When the king saw the men he said, "Who do you work for?"

"We work for the Marquis of Carrabas," said the men.

When the king left, Puss said to the men, "Who lives in that castle?"

The men said, "Our master lives there. He is an ogre."

31

Puss ran to the castle and knocked on the door.

When the ogre came to the door, Puss said, "Can I come in?"

"Come in," said the ogre.
He wanted to eat Puss.

Puss said, "Can ogres do magic?"

"Just look!" said the ogre. And he
changed into a lion.

35

"Is that all the magic you can do?"
said Puss. "Change into a mouse."

So the ogre changed into a mouse.

37

Puss jumped on the mouse and ate it! Just then, there was a knock on the door.

When Puss went to the door, he saw the king, the princess and his master.

"This is my master's castle," said Puss.

Soon, the princess and the boy fell in love. They were married and lived at the castle.

So the boy, the princess, the king and Puss in Boots all lived happily ever after.

How much do you remember about the story of Puss in Boots? Answer these questions and find out!

- What does Puss ask the boy to get him?

- What is the first thing Puss gives to the king?

- Who does the boy pretend to be?

- What does the ogre want to do to Puss?

- Why does the ogre let Puss into his castle?

- Which animal does the ogre change into first?

Look at the different story sentences and match them to the characters who said them.

"Is that all the magic you can do?"

"Our master lives there. He is an ogre."

"We must take you home."

"How can we earn some money?"

Tick the books you've read!

Level 3

Puss in Boots ☐	Angry Birds: Matilda Saves the Day ☐	Sharks ☐	Thumbelina ☐
Aladdin ☐	YOU won't like this present as much as I DO! ☐	The Elves and the Shoemaker ☐	

Jack and the Beanstalk ☐ | Furi on Music Island ☐ | Poppet Stows Away ☐ | Rapunzel ☐ | The Red Knight ☐ | The Jungle Book ☐ | Roxy and the Great Escape ☐

Hansel and Gretel ☐ | Harry and the Bucketful of Dinosaurs ☐ | Angry Birds: Bomb's Best Birthday ☐ | Angry Birds: Cheer Up, Chuck! ☐

Level 4

Dick Whittington ☐ | Knights and Castles ☐ | Peter and the Wolf ☐ | Pinocchio ☐ | I am Inventing an Invention ☐ | Harry and the Dinosaurs United ☐ | Heidi ☐

Katsuma and the Art Thief ☐ | Luvli and the Glump-a-tron ☐ | The Pied Piper of Hamelin ☐ | Sam and the Robots ☐ | Snow White and the Seven Dwarfs ☐ | The Wizard of Oz ☐ | The Little Mermaid ☐

Alice in Wonderland ☐ | Oddie The Hero ☐ | Angry Birds: Red and the Great Egg Off ☐ | Angry Birds: Stella ☐